The First Lunar Landing

Rodney Martin

Contents

Introduction

"I believe that this nation should commit itself to . . . landing a man on the Moon and returning him safely to Earth."

John F. Kennedy, President of the United States of America, 25 May 1961

This book tells how President Kennedy's words came true. When he made his speech, there was no spacecraft that could take people to the Moon and back. People did not even know if astronauts could eat, sleep or work in space. New spacecraft and equipment had to be invented. It took eight years to build the spacecraft and train the astronauts.

Apollo Spacecraft/Saturn V Rocket

The Apollo Spacecraft/Saturn V Rocket was as tall as a 33-storey building. The Saturn V had three main parts, called *stages*. The biggest stage had five rocket engines that together were as powerful as about 160 jumbo jet engines. If a home swimming pool was filled with fuel, these engines could suck it dry in about seven seconds.

The Apollo astronauts named their own spacecraft. The code names had to be words that would be easy to understand over the radio (lift flap).

The Astronauts

The astronauts (left to right): Collins, Armstrong and Aldrin

Three astronauts were chosen for the Apollo 11 team. They were Neil Armstrong, aged 38, Michael Collins, aged 34, and "Buzz" Aldrin, aged 35. Each astronaut was married and had children. Armstrong had been a test pilot, and Aldrin and Collins were pilots in the United States Air Force.

Training for the Journey

Collins in the simulator

The astronauts thought some of the training was interesting. They travelled to different places and met the people who made their spacecraft. They spent hundreds of hours in a simulator, which was like a smart video game where they could "crash" their spacecraft without getting hurt.

Sometimes they did not enjoy the training. One reason was they were often away from their families. Another reason was some of the training was very uncomforatble. For example, they disliked being spun around in a huge machine like the gravitron at an amusement park. They nicknamed this machine "the wheel".

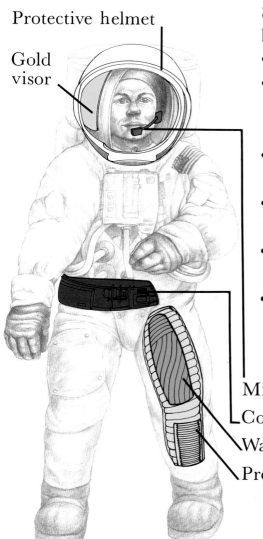

Protective helmet

Gold visor

Microphone

Control box

Water-cooled underwear

Pressure suit

An Apollo 11 spacesuit

Some things the astronauts had to learn to do:
- control their spacecraft;
- get into a spacesuit and move around without tearing it;
- eat, drink, sleep, and even go to the toilet in space;
- find their way in space by looking at the stars;
- use special television equipment and cameras;
- collect rock and soil samples.

Journey to the Moon

Apollo 11 launch, 16 July 1969

The astronauts expected the journey to the Moon
and back to take eight days (see *Apollo Mission
Profile* on back cover).

What happened during a day in space?

Morning (Spacecraft) Wake-up Call

The ground controllers woke the astronauts on the radio and told them news about their favourite sport teams, about their families, and about what was happening on Earth. The astronauts sucked on plastic tubes of coffee and chewed small cubes of bacon for breakfast.

Tasks

The astronauts checked their course by looking at the stars. They used computers to keep on course. All the equipment had to be checked in case it had been damaged during the launch.

They broadcast television pictures back to Earth. People all over the world watched the three explorers showing what it was like to be weightless. Collins poured some water into a spoon, then turned the spoon upside down: the water stayed in the spoon. Aldrin put some ham on a slice of bread, then made it drift across to another astronaut.

Sleeping

To sleep, the astronauts zipped themselves into hammocks, which stopped them from floating around and bumping into things.

Relaxing

When they were not busy the astronauts looked out the window or played music. Once they tricked the ground controllers by playing a tape of train whistles and noises.

 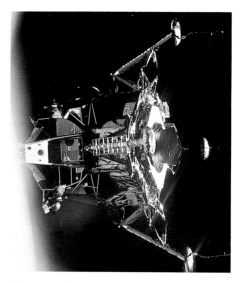

The Columbia as seen from the eagle

The Eagle as seen through the window of the Columbia

The astronauts travelled at about 40,230 km/h (25,000 mph) as they journeyed to the Moon. They made the spacecraft turn slowly as it travelled so the sun would not overheat one side of it. Collins called this the "barbecue mode".

Four days after the launch, Apollo 11 entered lunar orbit. Armstrong and Aldrin got into the Eagle, ready to land on the Moon. Collins stayed in the Columbia, ready to pick them up when they returned.

The astronauts talked to ground control as they

were landing on the Moon at a place called the *Sea of Tranquility*. This is what they said:

Eagle:	Coming down nicely . . . 200 feet, 4½ down . . . 5½ down . . . 5 percent . . . 75 feet . . . 6 forward lights on . . . down 2½ . . . 40 feet, down 2½, kicking up some dust . . . 30 feet, 2½ down, faint shadow . . . 4 forward . . . 4 forward . . . drifting to right a little . . . OK.
Ground control:	Thirty seconds.
Eagle:	Contact light. OK engine stop . . . descent engine command override off.
Ground control:	We copy you down Eagle.
Eagle:	Houston, Tranquility Base here. The Eagle has landed.
Ground control:	Roger, Tranquility. We copy you on the ground. You got a bunch of guys about to turn blue. We're breathing again. Thanks a lot.

As the Eagle was landing, it was heading for some huge rocks. Armstrong took control just in time and steered it to a flat place. All that practice in the simulator had paid off. The ground controllers were worried because when the Eagle landed it had only about twenty seconds of fuel left.

At Work on the Moon

Aldrin climbing out of the Eagle

Armstrong and Aldrin were supposed to sleep for a while after landing on the Moon, but they were too excited. So they helped each other into their spacesuits. Almost four hours after they had landed, Armstrong climbed out of the Eagle.

When Armstrong took his first step on the Moon, people all over the world stopped work or stayed up at night to watch him on television.

Aldrin setting up equipment to study the sun's rays

Armstrong and Aldrin worked on the Moon for two hours and twenty minutes. Some of their jobs were:
- to collect Moon rocks and soil samples;
- to set up a machine to measure moonquakes;
- to set up an experiment to study the sun's rays;
- to set up a mirror so a laser beam sent from Earth could measure the distance between the Earth and the Moon.

Returning to Earth

Eagle returning from the Moon

Nearly twenty-two hours after landing, the Eagle blasted off the Moon and back to the Columbia. Collins was excited to see Armstrong and Aldrin again. He had used a telescope to look for Armstrong and Aldrin on the Moon, but he couldn't find them.

The engine was fired and they headed towards Earth. Everyone was very anxious then, because if the engine failed they would be left orbiting the Moon, unable to get home.

Divers getting ready to help the astronauts out of the Columbia

They jettisoned the service module and checked their course before reentering the Earth's atmosphere. Finding the right course was like trying to hit a pinhead with a dart from across the classroom. The spacecraft became very hot (about 2,800°C/5,070°F), but the heat shield protected the astronauts. Parachutes lowered the spacecraft into the Pacific Ocean, where the astronauts were picked up by helicopters. The journey had taken 8 days, 3 hours and 18 minutes.

Lessons from Apollo 11

The Moon, showing the Apollo 11 landing site

The Moon samples showed that the Moon is about as old as the Earth (about 4,600 million years old). Tiny coloured beads of glass were one of the things found in the soil samples. No sign of life was found on the Moon.

The Earth from space

The Apollo mission also showed us that in the future we could travel even further than the Moon. From their spacecraft, the astronauts learned how fragile and beautiful the Earth is. Armstrong said, ". . . the Earth itself is . . . an odd kind of spacecraft . . . You've got to be pretty cautious about how you treat your spacecraft."

Apollo Lunar Landings

Six Apollo missions landed astronauts on the Moon.

MISSION	LAUNCH DATE	ASTRONAUTS
Apollo 11	16 July 1969	Armstrong Aldrin Collins
Apollo 12	14 November 1969	Conrad Bean Gordon
Apollo 14	31 January 1971	Shepard Mitchell Roosa
Apollo 15	26 July 1971	Scott Irwin Worden
Apollo 16	16 April 1972	Young Duke Mattingley
Apollo 17	17 December 1972	Schmitt Cernan Evans

Apollo 13 was unsuccessful.

Index

Glossary

code names Words used to keep radio messages short and clear. *Eagle* is shorter and clearer over radio than *lunar module*.

escape tower A rocket that would lift the astronauts to safety if the Saturn V did not launch properly.

gravitron A large machine that spins, pushing anyone or anything inside it away from its centre. The gravitron at an amusement park holds people against its walls as it spins.

heat sheild A covering on the outside of a space-craft that stops the spacecraft from burning as it reenters the Earth's atmosphere.

Houston The place in the USA where the ground controllers were based.

jettison To throw away something that is not needed.

launch vehicle A rocket used to lift a spacecraft outside the Earth's atmosphere.